Rocco the Rescue Stud

STEAK IN A BOWL

Written by Rachel Smith and Charlie Ford

Illustrated by Rachel Hathaway

Also available to buy from
www.roccotherockstar.com
or Amazon:

Rocco the Rock Star

Rocco the Rock Star and the Flower of Sascut

Rocco the Rock Star Swallows the Moon

Rocco the Rock Star and the Case of Mistaken Identity

Plus on Amazon only:
Rocco's Totally Pawsome Coloring Book for Dog Lovers
Let your little artist bring Rocco the rescue dog and his pawsome pals to life. Full of cute, pretty and heart warming original illustrations of dogs that will engage and entertain for hours.

First published in the UK in 2023 by Smith and Ford, UK.

Text © Rachel Smith and Charlie Ford 2023. All rights reserved.

Design and ilustration © Rachel Hathaway 2023. All rights reserved.

ISBN: 978-1-9163488-7-5

Rachel Smith and Charlie Ford have asserted their right under the Copyright, Designs and Patents Act 1988 to be identified as the author of this work.

This is a work of fiction. Names, characters, businesses, places, events and incidents are either the products of the author's imagination or are used in a fictitious manner. Any resemblance to actual persons, living or dead, or actual events is purely coincidental.

All rights reserved. No part of this publication may be reproduced, stored in a retrieval system or transmitted in any form or by any means, without the prior permission in writing of the publisher, nor to be otherwise circulated in any form of binding or cover other than that in which it is published without a similar condition, including this condition, being imposed on the subsequent purchaser.

Enquiries relating to reproduction should be sent to the authors at
info@roccotherockstar.com

www.roccotherockstar.com

Contents

Chapter 1
Here comes Suzi! — 6

Chapter 2
Playdate pals — 9

Chapter 3
Where the wind blows cold — 12

Chapter 4
A rollercoaster of a day out — 16

Chapter 5
A Roman race around town — 19

Chapter 6
A Royal encounter? — 23

Chapter 7
What lies behind the Yew Tree door? — 26

Chapter 8
A stranger shares the secret to happiness — 29

Chapter 9
Miss Andrews saves the day — 33

Let's meet Rocco the Rock Star and his *Pawsome Pals*

Rocco is an engaging little rescue dog who was found on a rubbish tip in Romania before being sent on the Happy Bus to his forever home with his Mummy in the Cotswolds.

Suzi is a lively loving Whippet cross and the newest member of the Rocco the Rock Star pack.

Flo is a big cuddly Bear with huge brown eyes, who was rescued from a farm and is now enjoying a wonderful life with Mummy and Rocco in the rolling Cotswolds Hills.

Sassie Snowdrops is a stunning Husky cross with sparkling blue eyes. She's smart and sassy, hence the name!

Jasper is an adorable Jack Russell Terrier who due to an illness in his younger years no longer has any eyes. Don't feel sorry for Jasper though – he is a brave little chap who just gets on with life and is an inspiration to us all!

Chapter 1
Here comes Suzi!

Rocco was sat in the window looking intently at the garden gate. He was waiting for Charlie, who he knew would come bowling through it at any minute with her big goofy smile, swinging a lead ready to take him out on another fabulous adventure.

Flo was happily snuggled down in her basket. She wasn't keen on going out in the mornings, preferring an afternoon stroll around town, ideally about half past three when the children were coming out of school and would be excited to see the teddy bear dog. Flo didn't mind being called the teddy bear dog – it often came with the toss of a treat or a little ruffle of her fur!

As Rocco watched, the gate suddenly swung open and a whirlwind of a dog came flying through it heading at full pelt straight for the front door.

Rocco jumped off the windowsill and launched himself at the new arrival. Charlie struggled to get

inside without tripping over them both as they charged around the living room, jumping over and under the furniture, ending up in a growling heap on the rug.

Flo was not amused. Who was this little upstart, she thought, and where were her manners? You don't just go bowling into someone else's house without so much as a good morning or good afternoon. Flo growled at the tiny dog and showed her teeth – she was going to teach this new pup some manners!

Suzi, the new arrival, realised her mistake and quickly rolled over, legs in the air, in an attempt to say sorry. Flo decided to give her the benefit of the doubt. She was just a silly young thing, Flo thought, and snuggled back down.

Suzi was rather relieved. She'd never seen such a big, scary dog but, oh boy, she did look so cuddly! Suzi hoped that one day they might be friends, but for now she thought she'd better calm down. She ran into the kitchen where Charlie was handing out treats. I rather like Rocco HQ, Suzi thought, I'll come again.

Chapter 2

Playdate pals

The following day, Rocco could hardly sit still on the windowsill because he was so excited at the thought that Suzi might come running through the gate again. He loved Charlie and he loved their adventures, but yesterday had been so much more fun. He'd loved having someone to run and run with.

Rocco loved it when his friend Sassie came on their adventures, but she only ever wanted to play chase, knowing with his rather short little legs he'd never catch her. He'd yelp to ask her to slow up but she'd just say, "Oh Rocco, really you can't catch me, I give up, I'm going to go and see Charlie for a treat and a cuddle," and he'd be left standing there. But with Suzi yesterday they'd run and rolled, and run and growled, and he'd bit her ear and she'd nipped his leg. All play fighting of course, but just so much fun!

Flo watched Rocco watching the gate, all fidgety and excited, and thought how sweet he was. She was too old to play with him of course, but she had grown to love him very much. As long as that Suzi didn't knock her over or get in her basket, Flo didn't mind her coming over again.

The gate squeaked open and, oh my gosh, Rocco couldn't believe it! Here came Suzi again, she seemed even faster today, racing across the cobbles towards the front door. She scratched and scratched the door until Charlie, who was running behind her trying to catch up, opened it and in they came.

Mummy won't be best pleased when she gets home and sees all those scratch marks on her front door, Flo thought to herself, she likes her cottage just so – that dog needs to learn some manners. Flo looked at Charlie as if to say, "Charlie, are you going to teach that pup some manners, or do I have to start growling again?" Charlie got the message. "Come on little Suzi, come into the kitchen," she said. "Please sit down and be calm and I will give you a treat."

Suzi soon got the hang of it and learnt to come and to sit and to keep out of Flo's way. Rocco had to admit he was rather impressed, she seemed a very quick learner for such a little pup. He reckoned she

was only a few months old, but boy was she on it! He really hoped she'd become part of the Rocco the Rock Star pack.

"Come on Suzi, come on Rocco, let's go!" said Charlie. "Let's leave Flo to enjoy her pâté filled chew toy in peace." Yes, do, thought Flo, and then I'm going to have a little nap and I'll join you all later round town.

Chapter 3
Where the wind blows cold

The next day was a special Sunday so Flo was up and out of her basket, doing her little 'let's go for a walk' wiggle as Mummy came down the stairs. Mummy laughed as Flo nuzzled the back of her knee. Rocco was jumping up and down, desperate to get out and start the day's adventures.

"Come on then, gang," Mummy said, "let's go join up with Charlie and the others. Today we are going to have an amazing day out in Stow-on-the-Wold."

Outside the gate they heard a 'beep, beep'. That's Charlie, Rocco thought, and he ran around in circles barking to let everyone know it was time to go.

Rocco was delighted to see not just Jasper and Sassie Snowdrops in the jeep, but stretched up in the front seat with her paws scratching at the window was Suzi.

Mummy sat with Suzi on her lap, who seemed suddenly to have fallen in to a deep slumber.

Rocco hoped she'd wake up and start being fun again when they got to this place they were going with a funny name.

About an hour into the journey, Charlie stopped for petrol and Mummy went to buy some treats, leaving the gang in the jeep.

"Where is it we're going?" asked Jasper. Rocco couldn't remember the name, but Flo was quick to answer. "I can't tell you how excited I am! We are going to Steak-in-a-Bowl, Jasper! Can you imagine, steak in bowls everywhere! I'm so looking forward to it."

"Did you hear that, Sassie?" Jasper repeated in the back of the jeep. "We are going to Steak-in-a-Bowl!" Sassie's eyes widened, she loved a bit of steak. Oh yes, that would be fabulous. Rocco just hoped the steak wasn't well done. He loved his Mummy but she had a habit of cooking everything until it was dark brown. He'd tried walking away from his bowl, but then he felt mean so he'd go back and eat it. Mummy said she worried about germs, so had to be sure it was cooked through, whatever that meant. Rocco thought back to when he lived on the streets

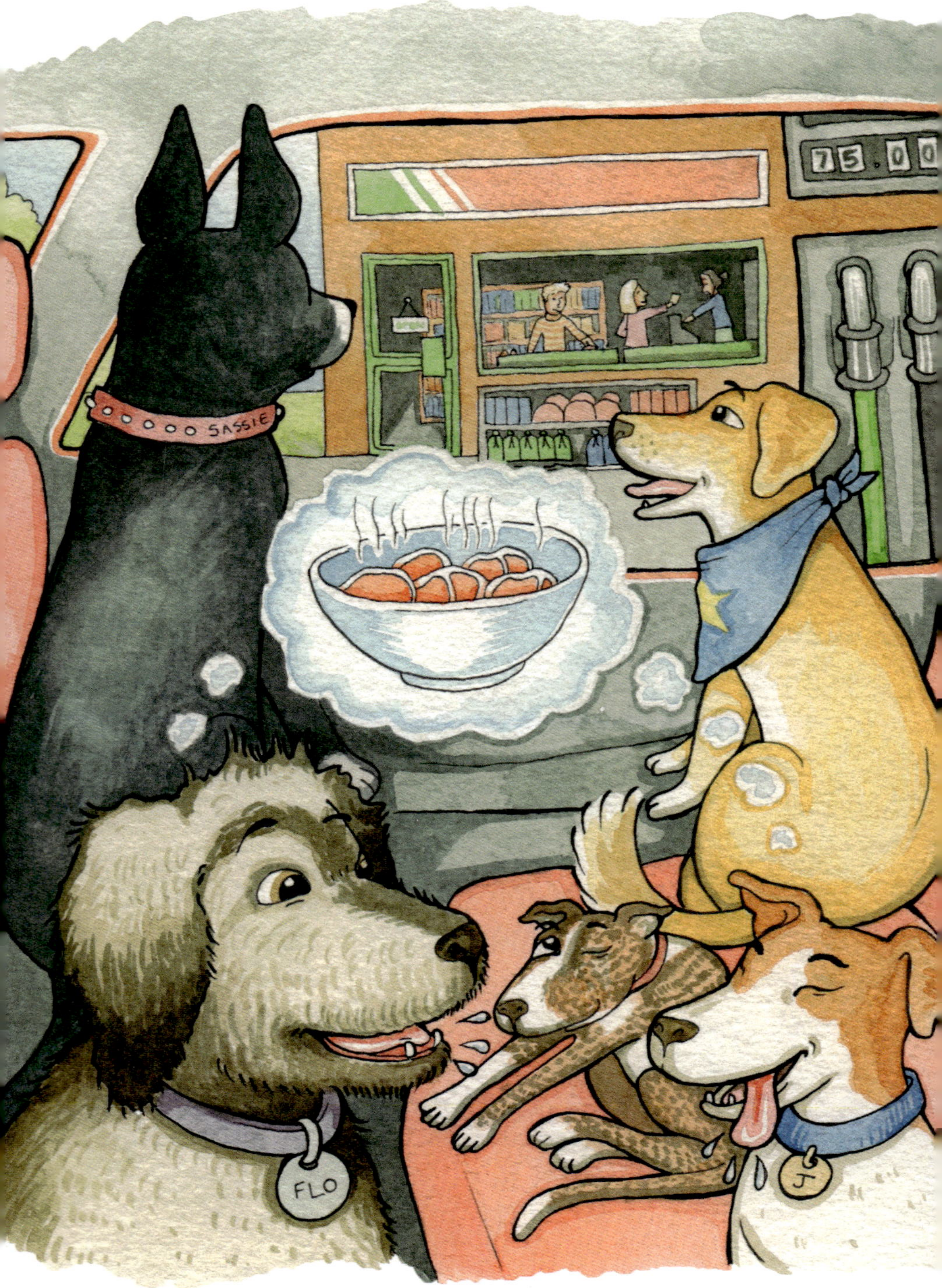
SASSIE
FLO
J

– no steak then, just the odd raw mouse… No, he really shouldn't complain, however this steak was cooked he would eat it. He looked at his Mummy coming out of the petrol station and he smiled – he really was a lucky boy, just like she said.

When Mummy and Charlie got back in the jeep they couldn't believe how excited the gang were to see them. "We've only been five minutes!" Mummy said, laughing as Rocco was licking her face and wagging his tail like crazy.

Suzi woke up, sensing the excitement and thinking they were there, but she soon realised they weren't so she settled back down again. What a strange bunch, she thought, but she really liked being with them and she was determined to make friends with the big furry one.

Chapter 4
A rollercoaster of a day out

"Heeeere we go!" exclaimed Mummy, waking Suzi, who was sleeping on her lap, up with a start. "Ooh, it's just like being on a rollercoaster," she added laughing, as Charlie drove the jeep down

the steepest hill Rocco had ever seen and back up the other side. Rocco couldn't help but mirror her excitement and wagged his tail excitedly setting off a Mexican wave of waggy tails in the jeep.

Flo couldn't help but lick her lips, she could almost taste that steak now! Jasper, too, was so excited he started to whine in the back of the jeep.

Really, thought Sassie, such a fuss. She much preferred it when it was just her and Charlie on the common with a ball, although she had to admit she *was* getting a bit peckish.

With a crescendo of excitement the jeep came to a stop in a really pretty market square with some rather elegant-looking town houses and shops around it. "Calm down everyone," said Mummy, "or no-one's getting out."

"Leads on gang," instructed Charlie, "let's go and explore!"

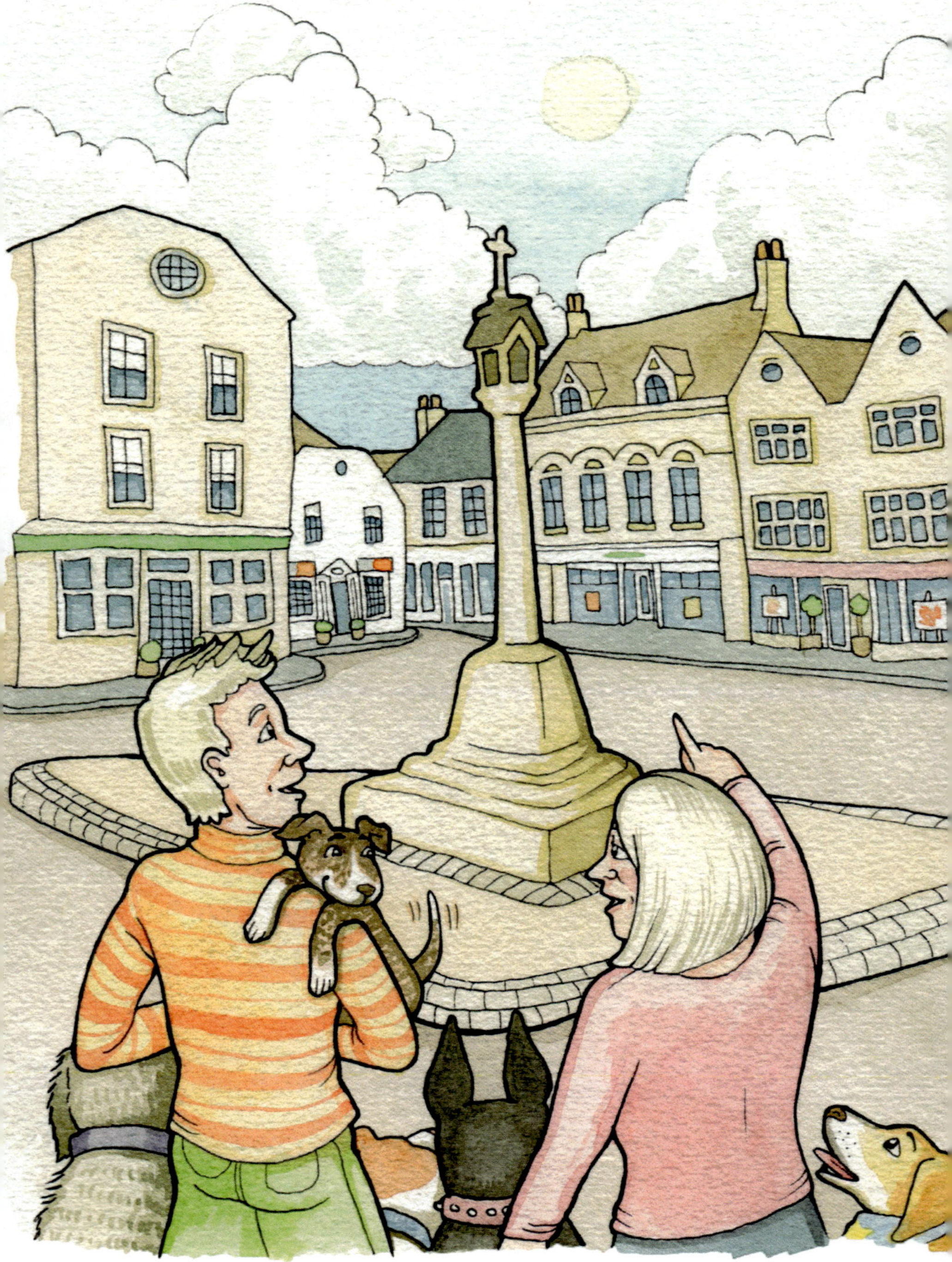

Chapter 5
A Roman race around town

After about an hour of walking around the narrow, winding streets, full of antique and coffee shops, the gang were starting to wonder where these bowls of steak were. All of a sudden Suzi stopped dead in her tracks and her ears shot up. She couldn't believe her eyes! All lit up in front of her in the centre of the shop window was a big, brass bowl, which she presumed was full of steak. Finally!

Before anyone had chance to stop her, Suzi launched herself into the shop, grabbed the bowl between her teeth and ran out – almost knocking a very grumpy Flo off her feet as she flew past.

Rocco was all up for a game of chase and he dashed after Suzi in hot pursuit.

"Stop!" shouted Charlie, but Suzi wasn't listening! She was having too much fun as she weaved in and out of the shoppers before veering off through the churchyard, stopping briefly to have a quick sniff of the most amazing door she'd ever seen.

Then off Suzi went again, back out onto the street, checking behind her for the rest of the gang to see if they were catching up. Just as Suzi was thinking she'd have to up the pace because Rocco was gaining ground on her she turned back around and – whoa, bang – she ran headfirst into the stocks!

Rocco and the gang pulled up quickly, stopping just in time to see the bowl go flying through the air. It narrowly missed an elderly gentleman who was sat on the bench just about to eat his sandwich.

Flo stared intently at the bowl, which was now upside down on a pile of grass. Disappointment flooded through her as she saw the elderly

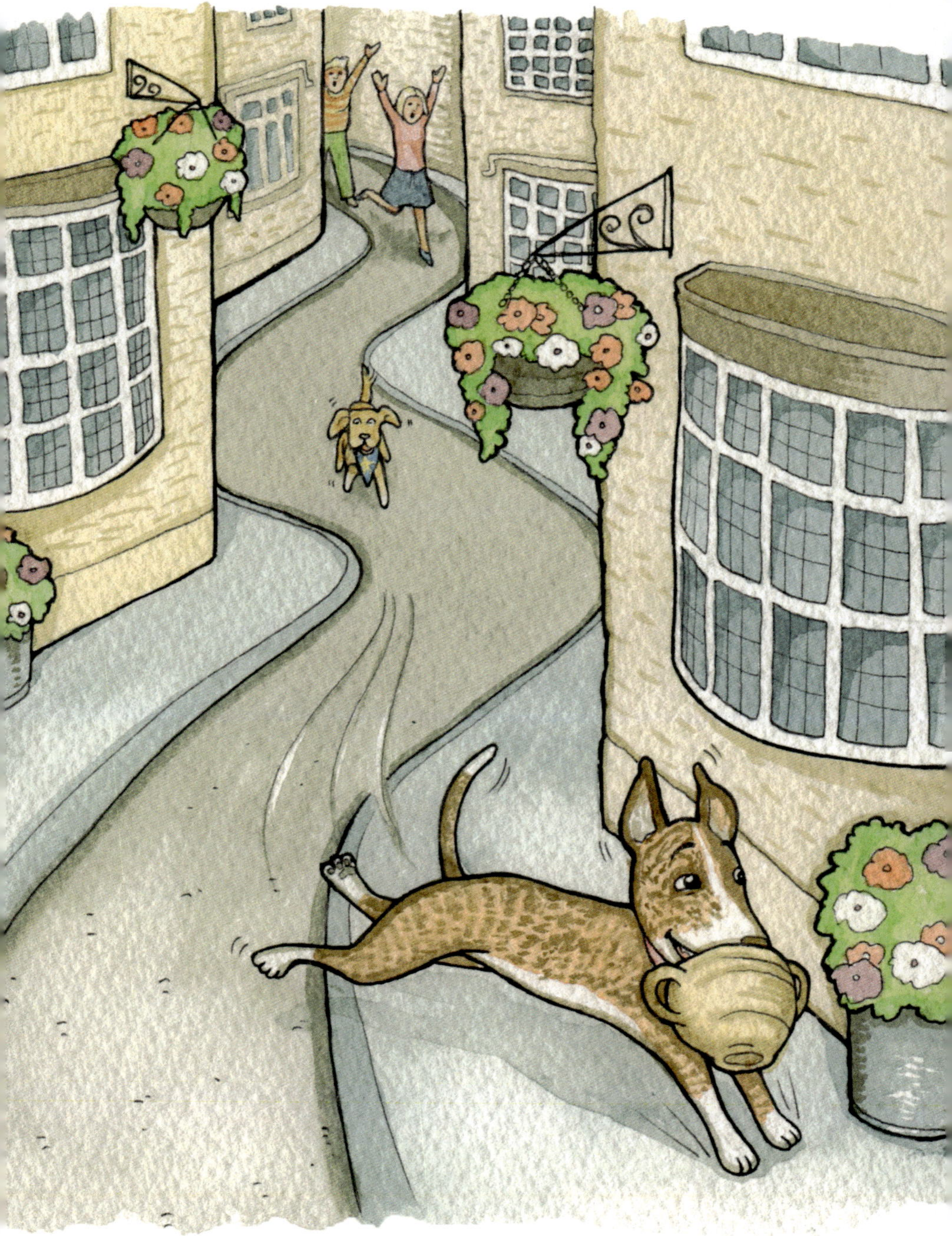

gentleman bend down and pick it up – it was empty! No steak anywhere.

Sassie burst into laughter as she saw Suzi's bum in the air and her paws in the stocks – served her right, Sassie thought, she was so naughty.

Rocco was just loving the whole experience, what fun, he loved a good game of chase – he missed that. When he was on the streets in Romania he used to have to chase the mice and anything basically that moved that was potential breakfast or dinner. Although he was very grateful to have his dinner put in front of him these days he did miss the thrill of the chase.

Chapter 6
A Royal encounter?

"Is this yours, madam?" enquired the elderly gentleman as he dusted off the bowl and handed it over to Charlie, who was frantically trying to get Suzi out of the stocks.

"Oh, thank you Sir," Charlie gasped. "I'm embarrassed to say it's not mine, my very naughty puppy Suzi here thought it was a toy and grabbed it from a shop window. We've been chasing her ever since."

Suzi rolled her eyes sorrowfully upwards and pulled her ears down and back as she tried to wriggle out of trouble and out of the stocks, but to no avail – she was well and truly stuck. She started to whimper softly. Rocco and his pawsome pals looked on worriedly.

"Oh dear," said the gentleman kindly, "I think one needs some help here." With that he raised his right arm, pulled back his suit jacket and he seemed to

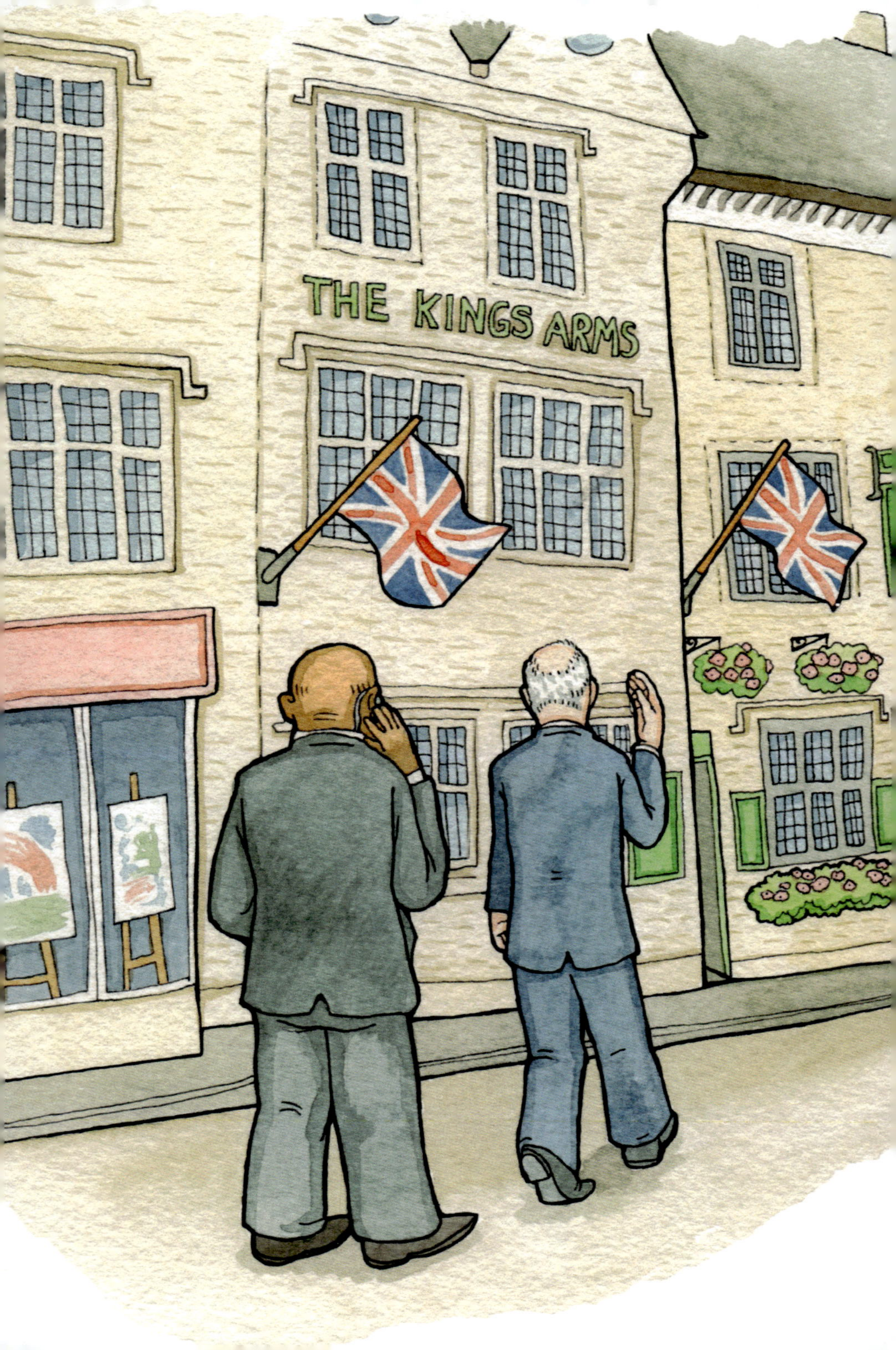
THE KINGS ARMS

press on his cufflink as he rotated his wrist. Then, out of nowhere, appeared a tall, burly man.

"Yes Sir?" he said. "How can I help?"

"Scott, would you be so kind to help this young pup out of the sticky situation she has got herself into?"

Scott bent down and in no time at all managed to release Suzi from the stocks.

Suzi was very relieved to be out of trouble, although she had rather enjoyed being the centre of everyone's attention. Rocco was just looking at her in complete adoration.

Charlie turned round to thank the elderly gentleman and to introduce herself, as she didn't even know his name. Unfortunately, he was already halfway down the street, heading towards the Kings Arms, but he did manage a wave as she called out "Thank you so much Sir!"

Chapter 7
What lies behind the Yew Tree door?

"Jasper! Jasper!" called out Charlie in a bit of a panic, suddenly realising now that Suzi was free from the stocks that Jasper wasn't behind her. Charlie scanned the square, looking for a little Jack Russell cross with no eyes.

"Don't worry, he won't have gone far. Let's retrace our steps," said Mummy softly, still trying to get her breath back from the chase.

So off the gang went again, Suzi in tow with her head down, knowing she was not in Charlie's good books. A beaming Rocco padded along beside her. He loved his new friend, she was so much fun!

As they walked back through the churchyard calling out

Jasper's name, they saw the most magnificent Yew Tree door. It was open, so in they went.

As the door banged shut behind them Rocco nearly jumped out of his skin. Suzi shuddered as a cold wind seemed to brush past her. "Rocco," she whispered, "I don't like it in here, shall we make a run for it?"

Although Rocco was, he had to admit, a bit scared, he didn't want to get into more trouble so he stood firm behind Sassie and refused to budge.

"Jasper!" Charlie called out into the darkness. "Jasper, are you in here?" Suddenly, out of the shadows appeared a man all dressed in black. "Can I help you?" he asked in a deep, solemn voice.

"Oh, yes please," piped up Mummy bravely. "We are looking for our dog Jasper. He's a Jack Russell, black and white, about so big?" she said, holding her hand out above the ground to show Jasper's height.

"Come with me," said the man, walking off briskly. They all followed him rather sheepishly. "Here we

are, is this the little chap you're looking for?" said the man, as he opened a rather creaky old door into a much brighter room, where Jasper was sat in front of a roaring fire. He was being hand-fed what looked like a bacon sandwich by a very jolly-looking lady.

"Oh yes," exclaimed Charlie with a little sigh of relief, "that's him, that's Jasper."

Jasper wasn't sure he wanted to go home yet. He was having a lovely time and thought he would happily sit there for the rest of the afternoon away from all the drama… but Charlie had his lead on him in two seconds and marched him out, while she said sorry lots of times to the Vicar and his wife for disturbing them.

Chapter 8
A stranger shares the secret to happiness

"Come on gang, now we've found Jasper we'd better take this bowl back to the shop and say sorry," said Charlie, feeling relieved but a bit worried at what lay ahead.

Charlie was right to be worried, the Shopkeeper wasn't best pleased! Luckily the bowl wasn't damaged. It turned out to be a Roman antique that was very old and valuable, which is why it had been placed centre stage in the Antique Shop window.

Suzi was only a pup, Charlie explained, and very naughty. Yes, she would agree to take Suzi to puppy training and, yes, she knew she needed to learn some manners – Suzi that was, not Charlie.

While Charlie was being as nice and smiley as she could be to try and win the Shopkeeper round, Flo and the gang were outside the shop waiting.

Flo caught the eye of a very shiny black dog who was looking curiously at them. "Can I help you?" Flo asked, her head tilted to one side and her big brown eyes staring intently at the stranger.

"Hola! My name's Val and I'm just wondering what you and your pawsome pals have been up to?"

Flo rather warmed to Spanish Val, she liked her calmness and her lovely shiny coat and her rather lovely accent. She told her all about their adventure with Jasper listening on, thankful for the explanation.

"Oh my," said Val, "you are all such fun but you do know you aren't in Steak-in-a-Bowl, you are in Stow-on-the-Wold?"

Flo couldn't believe it! Who had told her they were going to Steak-in-a-Bowl, was it Jasper? It normally was him that led them on a wild goose chase. Talking of Jasper, why was he staring at her so intently? He might have no eyes, but he was "looking" straight at her. Finally, the penny dropped and Flo realised with embarrassment that it was HER that had started off the rumour.

"Oh, I'm so disappointed Val, I really thought there would be bowls of steak everywhere," Flo said, her shoulders drooping as she realised her mistake.

"Well," said Val, "I used to be disappointed all the time when I lived in Spain. I was on the streets you know, with no shelter. Sometimes it was so hot and I was so hungry and so thirsty, but now I'm grateful for my comfy bed and my clean blanket. Although I don't get steak, I have lots of lovely food and cuddles and I'm so glad I was rescued."

Flo suddenly felt really bad, she was lucky too and she should be grateful, she'd had it even worse than Val when she was chained up outside in all weathers guarding the farm with cardboard for food!

How could she have forgotten that already and expected steak for her dinner?

"Val, you are so right," Flo said. "Like you, I am a rescue and I'd forgotten for a minute how bad I had it, thank you for making me remember and realise how lucky I am."

"No problem, my friend," Val said, "be grateful and you will be happy!" With that she was gone, leaving a lasting impression on Flo, who hoped she'd meet some more Spanish rescue dogs soon because they were so cool.

Chapter 9
Miss Andrews saves the day

"Well, what a day we've had," said Mummy as they began the journey back home.

Suzi was once again fast asleep – Rocco couldn't believe how she went from completely manic to a deep slumber within seconds.

"Shall we stop on the way home and see Miss Andrews, Charlie, as she might know some puppy trainers?" Mummy added.

"Yes, let's do that," Charlie answered enthusiastically. "Miss Andrews might have some wise words for us all and maybe some eggs for our tea."

Flo caught herself mid-thought – she had been thinking "Eggs? I wanted steak!", but then she remembered Spanish Val's advice – eggs will be lovely, she thought, and Miss Andrews always had a treat to hand… Flo found she was feeling happier already – this being grateful really worked!

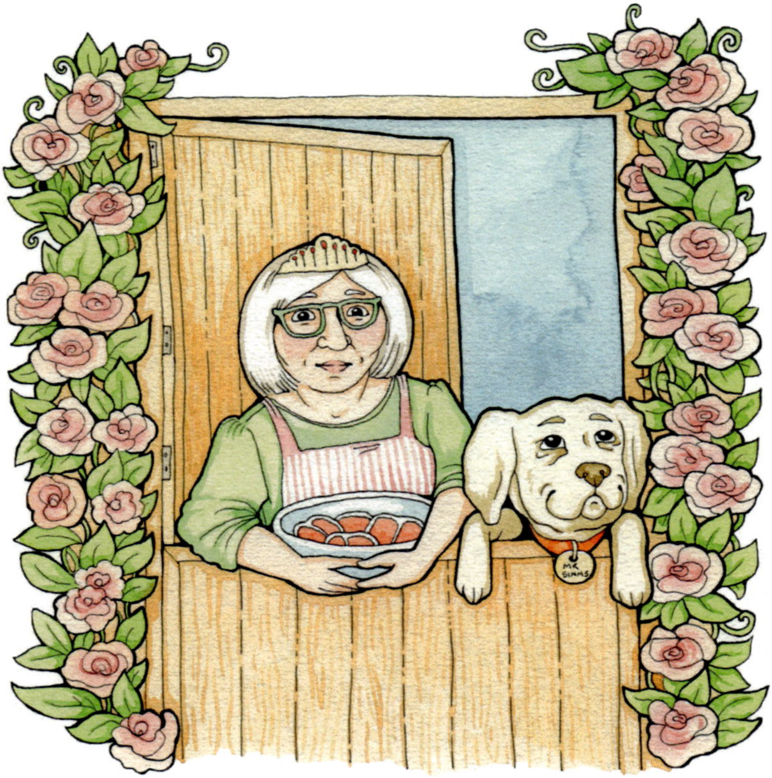
MR
SIMMS

Rocco started jumping around in the back of the jeep as they approached Miss Andrews' house. He loved going for walks with her dog Mr Simms and Miss Andrews was one of his favourite people.

Shortly after, they all piled out of the jeep and there was Miss Andrews at her gate with Mr Simms peering over the half door, treats in hand. Actually, Flo noticed, today she had a big bowl in her hand.

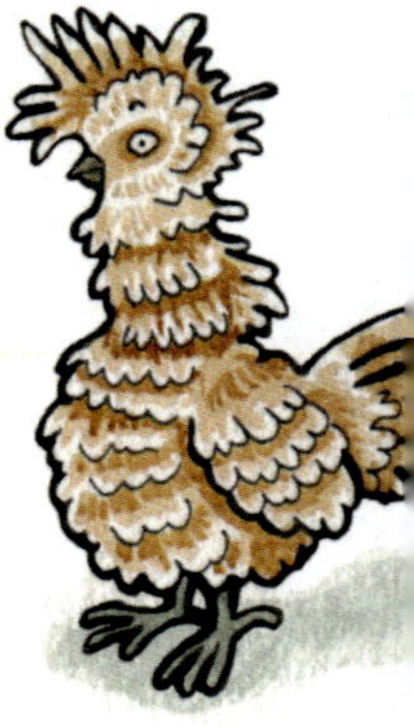

"Hello gang, how are you all?" Miss Andrews smiled. "I was just cooking a stew and I've got all this steak left, do you have time to stop for tea?"

Flo beamed from ear to ear. Wow, I really am one lucky girl, she thought.

Gratitude is at the heart of this book.

This book often reflects on the characters being grateful. What does that mean? It means being thankful for what you have. That's a really positive thing to do, to stop occasionally and think about what you do have rather than what you don't have.

Make a gratitude tree like this one

At night, just before bed, try to think of one thing you are grateful for…

Cut a trunk out of brown paper

… write that down on a leaf and stick it to your tree

and leaves out of green paper

Think about what went well in your day…

Remember sometimes things don't go well, but life is like a rollercoaster. Flo and Rocco are proof that even when you're down, life can take a turn for the better and you'll soon find yourself back up.

Made in the USA
Las Vegas, NV
06 May 2024